DEMARCO!!

BY

DARRELL KING

You sicken me! You know that?'' Mum finally speaks out after a long drive in an uncomfortable silence.

Well, I really don't think she gives an F if I drive her nuts or not, neither do I. If I consistently make her mad, she deserves it, all of it.

What the hell is wrong with you?, for God's sake!

She suddenly bursts out enraged, startling me. I maintain my cool though, unmoved

"why are you looking through the dam window?! I'm talking to someone" she asked. I still say nothing. ""Mute, huh? She asked.

The mini-van suddenly stops. "Get otta my car boy". I turned to face her!

Her two calm countenances told me she had enough to deal with for the moment. But still, I couldn't help but spit out a "What?!" "Ya, you heard me, Dermaco Demetrius! " OUT OF MY CAR!" She spat. Surely, this woman didn't think through this before deciding

The son of a ….. Before I could finish my statement, she shot me down!..Dont curse in front of me!.."Glared"

"He asked for it". I corrected.

"He asked for it?" He asked for broken bones to lose some teeth and get a black eye? For a 14years old, you're too hot tempered, "mum said"

He asked for them? Stitches? He asked to get beat?

Her voice kept rising by each word. "He called me a lunatic!" And so you beat him hard to prove he could be right?

"The dude looked for trouble. I was hyper couldn't help but give him what he asked for"

"I've told you lots of times to hold your fist. Fights don't solve anything"

"No mum., I don't believe that because I beat his ass, he is gonna give me the respect I deserve"

"what's even your problem anyway? You beat much and don't talk much; you've been into lots of fights just this past few weeks. So the whole town is looking for your trouble? Why cant I get into your head?" you never told me what's going on with you".......She paused.

I stared at her blankly "Oh so you now cared about what is going on with me?" you wanna know? I retort.

"Oh sweetie, you know I've always cared about you...." she started drawing closer for a hug..I moved aside, "Please, don't mum"..I don't want your sympathy nor pity..You only cared about your bottles and boyfriends..You don't give a shit about...." ...shut your goddamn hole this minute before I smack the mad outta you!

You don't know what its feels to be a mum..you don't know what I've been through..You don't know how I'm tryna cope with you...

" she starts to break down.." you, you don't know me..

Dont you dare point your finger at me..I was sixteen when I had you..I don't know much."

Great! I'm so tired of this. She annoys me, I hurt her. We always end up being even in this game without achieving much..Mom was beginning to sob. I needed a dues ex machine that didn't include an apology because I needed to really drive my point home this time..I hated it when she came back late nights from the strip club where she work with strange men all drunk to stupor. When she starts her second job in the bedroom, the neighbors know there is someone having sex.

The next day, the latest gossips I have to deal with are so frustrating. And here she is again in self-pity. "Uhm..." I have to go to Trey's to get..." I interrupt the sobbing woman moment and in turn am interrupted "Oh you are now friends with Trey Coleman? " Good to know you're finally socializing." She quickly concludes, but I don't mind breaking her heart..Me? Coleman? Never!!...I'd rather date a pig..I can't hang out with him. She lets out a sigh, disappointed.

"wha-ya gonna do at treys then?"

"Science project," I simply tell her.

"sure you don't wanna come home first, freshen up?" I replied"No, I'm alright!"

"Ok the" she said..

I came down from her ill-earned automobile. One of her "clients" recently got it for her.she wouldn't have been able to afford it..

"Be home before ten gerrit?" "Ya" Don't you be roaming on the street again, hanging out with bad guys, gerrit? "Yes" and when you're hungry, don't eat weed but food, got that?..This woman is beginning to get me angry

I tried that only once, I won't tell her that I don't mind doing it again..sometimes I feel she's an hypocrite- a drug addict that wont let her kid do drugs..I stared at the five dollars in my hand..Mom wasn't always broke. She worked too hard to be broke- both at the stripper pole and on the men she brought home. Still staring at the money, I decided to try that stuff again..

You daydreaming on my words, son? Her question brought me back just when I was about remembering the feeling I had the last time I was high

"huh?" I answered unaware at first what she asked..

"Whatever, don't stay late and be careful..Bye" with that she drove off..

"Science project my ass" how could she be that clueless?!! I begin to walk aimlessly down the street, except I wasn't so aimless..In the past I always had all these walks to clear my head, now I was headed to get my new found lover "Marijuana".

The streets are not safe.

Flint has never been and 2011, this year is probably the worst. So when a mother lets her 14year old son wanders freely in the evening you wonder what sort of guts she has. I can't blame her though, I lied to her and she trusted me. It's her trust in turn that gives me my freedom. I've been robbed a few times, I never told my mom but she would sometimes notices the bruises.

Then she start to yell that I don't move around late evenings. But you cant keep a man down. With time she starts to soften, on the other hand, learn my lesson not to carry anything valuable along as I move around. Other times I get beaten, because I have nothing to give. Stupid criminals! What has a 14 year old has to offer?

I moved around the slightly deserted neighborhood, won't be long before gangs of bad assess start to appear in hidden corners.

Maybe I would hang out with Wales and his guys today. Maybe not, they regard me as a kid, either way, I don't like hanging out.

I love the solitude of my thought, the view of the city, the city "A not so pretty, unholy sanctuary to my mind." I love Flint, maybe because I haven't had the chance to see other places but I'm in love with home , though its insecure

"Hey?" I hear a cracked, loud voice call out

"I'm talking to you". I turn around to see and old guy by the wayside, by his physical features, I could tell he was more Caribbean than black. He had a long un-kept dreads disfigured and discolored set of teeth with long, rough beard. His outfit was loose, tattered torn and dirty. The light skinned man's face reflected hunger and loneliness. He is obviously homeless

"Wha-ya looking at boy?" he asks in a hoarse voice.

"The person who called me", I simply answer

"Wha-ya gat for me?"

I sigh disappointed at his question. This man is probably crazy. "Silver and gold I have none". I replied simply with an expressionless face.

"Yea, I know you aint gat silver nor gold", am asking for your papers, he states clearly.

"Oh, there's a bookshop down the…" he interrupted!

"Don't play with me boy. Give me your money!" he had approached me now. He saw a few paces from where I was standing with a reddened face and a stance that said he was going to pounce on me any second. As far as I was concerned, this man wasn't getting nothing from me tonight.

I slowly reached for my back pocket where my jack knife was. I don't mind cutting of an ear of a trouble maker even if he was elderly.

He must think I'm vulnerable because of my age. Last time I landed in juvenile, it was because I stabbed a guy who threatened me in the torso. When I was given bail, I started going to the gym during weekends, I secretly paid for boxing sessions funded from my mom's pocket. If she knew I stole from her, she never admitted it because she wasn't aware as she is also a careless spender, spending on shits. The boxing lesson was to help me defend myself better from danger because I also went home with some serious injuries too after that encounter.

I brought out my knife and took a stance, the man suddenly took back with fear slowly retreats away and raises both hands and run off.

"Coward," I muttered. It is so weird seeing a thief back off so easy at the sight of a knife, the man seems more like a beggar to me. If he suddenly wants to practice theft, he needs to get a heart and at-least a weapon..

Its getting late and I'm starving already. Cannabis would be for another day. I grab some fries and a diet coke and head home. I rushed up stairs to our apartment, as I entered into the apartment; I was greeted with the thick smell of cigarette and alcohol.

You're home early" mom says without emotion. "Ya," I replied

"Good night" she simply says.."You too.." with that I go into my room leaving her stoned in the living room. Well that was stony, my mum's personality when she's high. I call her stony because of her cold, reserved countenance. She just recoils back into herself and doesn't say much except making a few vague statements about the hell she went through with her dad and my ass hole of a father who I never knew.

Then she starts throwing and breaking things. If I'm not in her way, I don't get hurt. My mother has never attempted to hurt me physically except once while I was five years old and most probably when I was in her womb.

The way she most times makes me feel like a burden betrays the thought that she may have tried to get rid of me while I was a foetus or baby. I wish I knew why she didn't succeed but she is always too quiet or pissed for a proper conversation. I've never known this woman though I'm certain this wasn't how she used to be. Something must have died within her, someone killed her sanity and tortured her emotions deep down I still believed she craved love

Lying on my bed staring at the ceiling, I listened to the sudden silence, she must have finally turned off the Television getting ready for bed. The quiet is what I've been used to my whole life. The only time noise existed was when a certain kind of business was conducted on bed in next room. I got up and move over to sit by the window.

I look out staring directly into the flat just across the road. I flash-back to past years when I was still little. I had a friend in that apartment; she was still so far the best thing that ever happened to me. Kelly marcus gave my childhood a memory.

An angel sent to relieve a depressed boy only for her to move away two weeks before my ninth birthday, sending me back to the insignificant unmoving being I was. The marcus family had moved to New York, just like that. No prior notice and they never came back.

I sigh reminiscing on the little memories we shared. They were quiet blur now. It was a long time ago but I still hold on to those moments of fun and happiness all sponsored by one little girl. I wonder if she still thinks about me. Definitely not I guess. " Forget this".

I tell myself. She's gone for good. Don't long after what can't be yours. I retire to bed just as mum shuts the door to her room. Sleep came easy.

The next morning, I wake up with a serious headache. "What the hell", I half mutter to my self with a pained look on my face. I go out to get some aspirin when I catch a glimpse of my mum in the kitchen, before I could ask her how she got to the kitchen, the aroma of pancakes hit me..

"Wow!" I said to her.

"You like what's going on?" she asked

The last time she cooked was like three months ago and it wasn't without a reason so shoot!"

"Hmm, its nothing really. I got you a new psychologist"

The grin was wiped off my face, not replaced with a frown though but none at all. I wasn't shocked, though slightly surprised.

"But......I thought we agreed I wasn't mental anymore?" she rolls her eys

"Common, you know the difference between a psychologist and psychiatrist."

The lady is only going to cancel you for the time being since you have problems blending in and opening up except if it involves the fist. I don't think the previous ones I've hired in thepast, did their job well".

"Psychologist or psychiatrist, both make you feel you have something going wrong up in your head and I've told you I'm fine, mom". I have no problems, so stop injuring my ego.

"But you do have issues even if you insist there is no problem.

"Violence and anger issues".

You need to wake up to that".. her words merely stung my ears..

"I'm sorry if you feel I hurt your ego but that is only solution I can think of right now, you have to resume being counseled if you make progress, I promise you won't go back there".

"I don't wanna go meet any if those high headed folks. I love me the way I am".

"You love Juvi? You wanna go to jail because of some stupid ego" now listen to me, you have problem and instead of admitting that later in prison, we gonna try and help you now, its not too late!"

"I don't have problems" I yell at her.

"Oh, yes you do my hot headed son. Yes you do! Listening to your mom or good advice from older people suddenly seems to be number one her good advice does a drug addict have to give? Before I can take back my words which I actually couldn't, the sharp sting from a palms contact with my face is what I'm suddenly trying to soothe.

"Do whatever you want, it is not about me now, but about you, I'm gone, I don't want you to end up like me. I want you to be better. That's why I want professionals counseling you because I don't fit that role." It would be mere hypocrisy.But since you've chosen to use me as your role model, choosing to point fingers at my mistakes when I'm trying to correct you. Fine live your life the way you want it.

"without caution" she concluded with tears streaming down her checks. I am sorry momma I said with a truly sober reflection. She ignored me and placed a plate of pancake in front of me then walked away. I stared on them without the interest I previously had in them when I first walked into the kitchen. How could I eat when I stole someone else's appetite? I had to make things right. What the fuss about not taking counseling sessions all about? It wasn't gonna kill me to please my mum, it's just a ones thing.

She maybe unfeeling once stoned but when she is her real self, she shows how much she loves me. On the other hand, am really stiff necked, both in accepting or reciprocating anything except a punch. It wasn't like she even loved taking narcotics; it was all to get the bad experiences off her mind for sometimes.

She needed to be free and I wasn't making things easier for her. Mom use to be a lot worse while I was a kid, during those times of assault and constant hitting when social services threatened to take me away, she never showed concern or care towards me. Then, every moment she was high on either liquor or subnstance. She avoided me cause I bought her sad memories she neve wanted to disclose. Her behavior had influenced my boring up bring.

When the state threatened to take me away from her she pleaded I stay, she was assigned a psychologist. This regular check up led to change. Slowly, she became a better person, and accepted me into her life. Although, she didn't stoped drinking nor drugs but stopped the assault and began to show love but am used to her former self.

I am still adjusting to the new her considering she turned a new leaf only three years ago. I had to make things right, I don't see any effect those sessions with psychologist had but I was going to make my mum happy.

I walked into her room she was seated on her bed staring away from the door. Am sorry am not a mother figure she said. I have disappointed you but that shouldn't hinder you from doing the right thing. I understand and am really sorry if you hadn't completely dismissed the thought I had like to take those sessions I say. She turned around to face me smile plastered on her face

" you want to do this for me or for you" she asked

"for both of us" she replied

"give me a hug"

The subsequent days have been really idle considering the fact that I was on suspension from scholl. The first few times of my misbehaviors in the new school I went to, I was either given detention or a different punishment but now I have to seat my ass home and wait till the end of my tree weeks suspension.

I'm sure trying any shit gain would mean they have to let me go. I'm not bothered though school and academics sucks. My life is not going to be defined by an institution with only restricted, shitty knowledge to offer, and a bunch of ass-holes. Mum has been out since afternoon and now night was drawing near but she still wasn't back. It was beginning to cause me worried; I dialed her number a thousand times but was switched off. Something wasn't right; I was about leaving to the last place she said she'd be when my cell phone begins to buzz, I answered the strange number.

"Hello", I speak first.

"Good day sir", is this Beatrice Langley's resident? An elderly man's voice booms in.

"Y-e-ssss" I dragged my answer hoping it wasn't something bad I did replying.

"Well sir, there's been a murder." You are to come to over here to identify the corpse"

"What?!" "Wha-ya talking about?" confusion and fear in my voice.

The lady I earlier mentioned was mugged and shot in the chest by some unknown assailants. We need you to come to the Genesee county morgue, if you are related to the deceased, so as to …"

"Fuck! No!" I scream out in my frustration heaven let the phone slip out of my hand..

I stopped listening to the man from the part where he mentioned"shot in the chest." I stood against a wall punching, screaming and kicking it. "Fuck!" I scream again. I should have followed her. She wanted getting groceries from the store and now she's gone just like that. I sit on the couch palms on my face and cry my eyes out. Later that evening, I rushed to the contrary morgue and indeed confirmed it was her "I was inconsolable.."

Months passed like days. Six months had passed and I was a mess, uncertain about what my life would hence be like. I was a ghost living through time. So broke and broken, she was just starting to accept me into her life. I was just starting to appreciate what it felt to have a mother. Now I was going to have to get used to life without her face.

Have to live on my own full-time. Life has forced me to be a man. No more babysitting. Just responsibilities I wasn't ready for.

Today, most especially was a sad day for me. August 4th. As I take down another gulp of my liquor, I whisper "Happy birthday, mom" as tears roll down to my jaw line

Its winter, funny how time flies, last week was my 15th birthday. It was just like any other day, every other lazy day. Wake up, watch Tv, do exercise, get high. If there wasn't weed, I went down the street to purchased. I was ignorant, remained ignorant, locked myself behind walls that couldn't make me forget the memories I once had within them. Of course, I wasn't meant to forget, not as long as I remained there. Remained here..

I needed to go out but to where? I was cashless, alone, unhappy. An angry young man with no expectation. Even where I stayed was unaware of its inhabitant. Dirty, unkept and untidy described the apartment. I didn't give a damn who did? No one ever came around Christmas. It never meant much, but now it means nothing. Only the cold was what I could feel. I was numb but not immune to the cold and so I remained inside where it was safe until I couldn't take it anymore.

A man mad was hungry, you can't deny yourself of food. But where was the money? And the bastard who killed my mum, he or they, one person must have pulled the trigger though. H's probably chilling with some people this moment-laughing at a joke. I just wish I knew who. I wish I knew who made her silent, but wishes don't always come through.

Then, I came out on Christmas eve.

I was about to make someone's Christmas an unhappy one. That was at least what life gave me. If I was to share what I have with others as we've been encourage to do every Christmas, it would be sadness but I won't give that out. It was my cross to carry. I could only give unhappiness and it wasn't mu fault.. I guess

I stared at the deserted street covered in snow most shops would not open around this time of the year but the coffee shop. I could do it I'm just not sure a kitchen knife could do it. I approached, I take a peep to be sure there were no cops inside. No cops, few people. That's luck, I was bad at this, so I needed to be lucky. I had no experience in being a burglar so I needed to hang out with the guys. Needed orientation, but I couldn't get myself to doing so.

Sooner than later, I would end up killing someone if a situation called for it. Right now I only needed money, desperately, but not to the extent of committing murder. One would most definitely do that if you joined a gang.

I'd rather hand those bastards to the police than join them anyway. One of them killed the only family I had. I can't stand working with the same people. I am a thief by my own making. I refused to do menial jobs because I didn't have the experience, patience nor guts to apply for any.

I wear d mask. Let's see how this goes. I run in and point the knife at the receptionist, an old lady. She raised her hands above her head. I order her to give me all the money in the counter. I swiftly look back still pointing the weapon at her, it's a provision store. I should have known that at least before barging in, stupid. Not that it would change my determination. A few customers around stop to look at the drama going on. Luckily none was bold enough to approach me to collect the knife. "What tha hell y'all looking at!" I try to scare them off with the loudest bazz voice I could use.

"Here it is" the woman hands me the money. I don't wait to ask or confirm if it is all she brought out. I scurry off with the money which I took into a small strap bag I took along, as part of my intimidation. I took off my mask when I'm no longer within range of sight. I run as fast as

I came home when I spot people coming out of the store I was wrong, I was too scared to keep doing this. I needed to take up my responsibility. "I need a job." I let out the statement between heavy pants as I furiously shut the door.

But as time went on, I waved off the idea of getting a job once more. I yielded to the temptation of robbing another store and wasn't lucky this time. I was hit behind the head. When I regained consciousness, it was in a prison. Being behind bars wasn't a new thing for me. It was a familiar territory. It was getting out that is the problem who was going to bail me? I asked my self

Luckily enough, I was set free the following week. It had to do with the testimony those at the mini-market I intended stealing from gave. They said I seemed shaky while I ordered the attendant and suggested I should be allowed to go since I was a miner. I was huge and muscular but my face betrayed my age. It was so stupid of me trying to rob solo a shop again with a mere knife when I knew I was only lucky the first time.

I wasn't comfortable with the idea but I became a waiter, I had no choice.

The following year I was able to socialize with others a little based on the nature of my minial work. A waiter had to be nice and friendly. I was able to meet some guys whom I constantly hang out with. I can't call them friends yet but we drink, smoke and party together. I guess we share the same characteristics that exist in friendship. I never said much in their midst though, my constant quietness and beefy body probably gave them the idea that I was in my late teen. I was hanging out with guys quite above my age grade and they were clueless.

By February, I lost my job. A customer got the fist from me when he decided to poke his mouth into my affairs crossing his boundary. Without prior warning, my ass got fired just like that. My inconsiderate boss sacked me without a chance to explain myself.

The only means I had to survive- cut off like label from a new cloth.

"Well, fuck you very much." It was a headache working for you anyway and fuck everyone of you too.." I point at those innocently taking their lunch.."Yes". This is goddamn injustice. You all looking at me like you don't know...."

"Dermaco, get the hell out. You shouldn't still be here", I've paid you for the days you've worked for me so far now go calm yourself elsewhere and stop scaring my customers", he said calmly but friendly.

I was already shaking; finger clenched tightly and heart pounding fast. There was enough drama for the day, punching this stout man's teeth out would probably be for another day. I storm out in rage not without making one last statement though,"Watch your back man".

I say carelessly before leaving.

"Thanks", I hear him say"..and you too, bobby harshly". As I walk by the road I pour out all my anger on a wall, injuring myself in the process. What a nerve? Who the fuck does he think he is talking to a nigga that way? He'll sure get beat one of these days. Now how the hell was I supposed to pay for my rent which would soon expire?

Just then my cell comes alive. It's a message from Dre saying we should hang out at the usual bar/club that night and the other guys would be present. I replied with a text that I would be there. I take one last looks at the dinner I used to work at. I leave a sigh and walk away from it premises. By evening, my mood had improved entering the slightly over-crownded and noisy club, I say to myself "Thank God it's friday" I move to the bar where the others were.

"Watagwan man?" Rowan speaks first. I reply with a smile. "D-man, whats up?"

"I'm alive people.!!" I simply answer

I noticed martins outfit and almost role my eyes in exhaustion of the boring concept, "What's with you and yellow?" Are you an "Yellow ambassador?"

The others laugh as he replies that he only loves the color. After a few more jokes, it was finally time to tell how our day went. Each of us spoke and when it get to my turn..

"I got kicked out today". Fired ! There were some "Ohs" here, and "ahs" there

"Wha-yhu do?" Dre asks…

"Kicked a disrespectful mother fucker's ass". I only gave a lesson to the guy."

I defend, hands raised. Well, if he wasn't respectful, dude needed the lecture, Rawan said.

"So he fired you just like that" No appeal? Martins speaks

"I'm afraid so.

"The man needs a lecture too" says Dre

"Nah", I object

"Then we take his goods, his money"

"what?" I gave him the … "are you really serious look." "No", what are we now? A gang? I ask casually with a smile playing on my lips as I take a shot. They look at each other, puzzled.

We're always been a gang Dree" Rawan says

And you are our newest and youngest recruit. I heard someone else say

"You guys do…shit together?" I ask in slight shock. They all just nod their heads.

"Common don't sweat it. Another shot!" martins shout when the bartender came around. There was no need being nervous for now, I wasn't robbing yet if I was, it would be well planned, with the right weapon and people. I don't give a shit. If I was broke, I don't mind taking a rich dudes property.

"Wow" look at that. I'm gonna tap that ass"

And off Dre went..

"Hope smart here doesn't wear yellow at nights when you guys are conducting serious business?"

I joked, he gives a smile and replied "Not exactly"

By February, I wasn't so amateur in a burglar anymore. We know how we run things. "The strategies for not getting caught"

The organization and shit, but all I got was never enough to pay for my rent which was due in March. Two weeks and I got kicked out. No negotiations.

I didn't give it much thought since I had friends who I could squat with till I could get my own place. My former residence was shitty anyway; only good thing about it was the painful memory of my mum which I really wanted to get rid of as at now. I however, did not expect to be rejected by all.

Fucking silly excuses everywhere

These were guys I finally accepted as my friends. We did most of our shit together.

We defend each other and now I need their help the most, I'm suddenly a burden

I basically lived on the street though an old guy allowed me bunk with him for time being.

It was in a deserted building with lots of graffiti and filth. No one owns the place, so I guess the old man is crazy for "Letting me stay" with him. He has no choice; even robbers came there frequently to plan their next attack.

Most times I couldn't stand the place. People usually came there to take a dump while we weren't is. The smell of piss and fecal waste alongside decayed liquor was enough to get one's lungs damages but I had no choice. I needed shelter at night. In the day time I was always at a regular coffee shop I still didn't take time to check the name. all I knew was the people were nice and the service were good. They usually place a discount on their coffee which happened to be my new and only nutrition.

One day as I sit quietly sipping from a mug, I hear some girls talk about a minister coming to Atherton for a convention, I ignored them and while taking my leave after paying for the coffee. I saw a pretty girl walked into the shop "She had those assets complete". Damn! Marched with a radiant smile and shiny long hair, she takes a glance at me and looks away before I could think of what to say. She goes to order a cup of coffer while I just look on like an idiot. She finally turns around, coffee in her hands and notices me watching her "Can I help you?" she asked..

"Huh..no.....s-sorry." I quickly take my leave before I embarrassed myself any further. After walking a reasonable distance, I began to regret playing statue back at the coffee shop. Atleast I would have asked for her name, I just stood there hooked on my owns words that refused to come out, making a fool of myself.

I then take a good look at myself. I look like a beggar, I wasn't even presentable at sight so how did I plan to impress a lady. If I reeked, I did not know. I had become too familiar with the smell of filth in that fucking abandoned warehouse. I needed a clean-up at least. "A shave"," bath" and "new pair of jean and shirt".

I had to look better next time. I was able to get all those with the little money I had left, now I was damn broke once more, waiting and hoping everyday that the same girl walks in again but she never came back

Old habits don't always die. Once again, I found myself stealing from others to survive. This time though, I was breaking into homes when their occupant weren't around. I took anything light and valuable I could find and sold it.

It wasn't safe stealing from shops and supermarket like I used to do with my clique back then. We had guns, we watched each other back and funny enough, we carted away with much. I just don't know the money always disappeared quickly. Drinks, weed, parties

That was always what we invested in.."Fuck all of them". "leeches!"

I scream out while alone one day, "Those bloody parasites!" they suck you dry when you need "em most". I wasn't exactly sure who I was referring to. My friends?. Bitches? May all of them. But the thing I was now sure of "I ain't gonna be nobody's pussy anymore, won't be a fucking rat you can toil with or use " I spit the word staring wearily at the particular graffiti painting on the wall. I was drunk as hell. I was aware , but I still meant everything I said. People only used other people and then throw them out in the trust when they are done. I wasn't going to be used or dump anymore. I was the rat, giving my dudes the info they needed to carry out an operation. I was the ear on the street. I agreed to take the smallest share so there would be peace. I was their stupid errand boy and when a black brother had no place to stay they shut their doors against me. Not like any of them were squatters or had flat mates. They just didn't give a damn. I slowly fall asleep with my thoughts wide awake.

I continued to break into places whenever I was out of cash, sometimes merely escaping getting caught. Then one day I meet a man named Frank Albright. He was a Baptist minister who just came into town

He must have been the guy those girls were talking about. Any way we met by coincidence, his jeep developed a fault and I was able to fix it while his two moronic bouncer looked on. The man expressed his gratitude and offered me some money to show how thankful he was. I hesitate at first but accept it after some persuasion. What was a broke nigga to do? He then asks to drop me off at my house. I out rightly told him I don't have a home hoping he would just shake his head at me in pity and drive off but it was the opposite. Ever since, he became a pest. The man wants to adopt me. I don't know much about him but I heard he owns an orphanage home. I decided I wasn't going there. I didn't trust this very religious man of God. Well I should have stood rigid on my decision, despite him tailing me all the way to the dump where I lived to convince me to follow the lords pathway. I regret accepting to go to Lippincott with the minister to be part of the "Renewal center" although certain inevitable events led to it.

As at the time I was still conducting my hustle on the street, I came back one day only to find out the warehouse was about to be demolished. The demolitionists refused to tell me anything or who ordered the demolition. I was happy but I could do nothing.

I wander about without a destination, there was no other option than to sleep anyway. I had to figure something out tomorrow. I could not sleep well that night cause I had no direction nor hope, no one and nothing. Right now, I only had companions in mosquitoes and rats.

The next day, I still haven't figured anything out. I took shelter from the sun by jumping from one restaurant to another just like a stalker, the minister finally caught up with me.

"Dimarco!" he called

"It's Dermaco".

"need a ride" he offered

"no, I'm fine"

"you sure? Your face defines worry son"

"I'm not your son!" I counter

"I don't object. But how about we have a little talk?"

"we've had all the talk in the world and my answer remains NO. am a grown ass man…."

He chuckles at my last statement. I frown, already getting pissed, giving him a questioning look.

"really? Grown ass man and you are on the street".

This was getting tiring "all am saying is that I have a choice, stop treating me like a kid!"

"am sorry I really am. But do you actually have a choice?"

The question gets my mind racing. Do I have a choice.

"if you change your mind, you have my card". He then speeds off on that final note leaving me to sort out my options. Options? I had no other. Just one. "Shit" frustration had me.

I needed to quit being stubborn if I must be helped. The man has been so far nice to me. Taking one to have dinner with him on two occasions , "D-man, you have no option".

I search my back pocket for the card he gave me days ago. I go to the nearest payphone and dial the number printed on it.

It takes a while but then someone finally picks.

"Hello", I say

"Hello, can I speak to the minister?"

You have an appointment? The bold voices speaks again

"Well Derek or whatever your name is? you and I know minister aint busy right now." Ya! This is Dermaco and he just drove off right now, so give him the Goddamn phone!"

After some unintelligible noise, the minister finally speaks

"Has someone thought things through?" he immediately asks.

"Yes."

"What's your conclusion?"

"Yes"! finally push the word out after a pause

"Great!" I'll be going back tomorrow so you can come to my suit at Holiday Inn hotel and spend the night if you wish.

"So, what?" A couple now? No, thanks pick me up tomorrow where you left me today around 8am"

"Are you serious?" He asks, concern in his tone

"I sure am, bye, sir" and I hang up.

The next day, 7:30am, I was already by the payphone, awaiting patiently for his land Rover to come around. He came in a different brand though. I hop in and we start the drive back to Lippincott. There are two more escort vehicles behind us.

"Don't worry, marco you gonna love the renewal center, he says with a smile patting my shoulders" I don't reply but pray he is not wrong.

The Albrights mansion wasn't so detached from another fairly large building beside it. It was guessing it was the boy's home. As we arrive, the minister is welcomed by members of his family which were just his wife and mother. The rest were his servants, house maids and some church members. He dismissed them all later and introduces me to his wife, a fat, unattractive woman as the new "Son" Dermaco Demetrius. She welcomes me warmly with a grin and handshake.

The woman introduces herself as "First-Lady"

"Emma Albright"

"Nice meeting you", was just my reply.

"Come in boy, I've chosen a delicacy for dinner and I know you'll love it"

"Oh-Kay", I shyly reply with a nervous smile. As we go in, I cant help but notice how beautiful the house was. I looked around, jaw hanging apart from each other. This is surely the prettiest place I've seen physically. Lady emma and I have a chat for a while before dinner is served. She asks some questions about my background which I answer quite frankly.

"Wow, where do you get those muscles?" she teases rather flirtingly which surprises me

"Exercise"

"Cool".

The chef finally comes and serves what we've all been waiting for. "Bon appetite", he says before taking his leave. We are all seated, ready to dig in after a prayer said by the pastor. Mrs Emma proved herself to be a glut- talking excessively and consuming her meal in a rather exasperating manner.

The pastor showed his displeasure on his face but his wife went on without a brother, obviously not noticing her husband's countenance. Soon it was time for me to go. She gave me two shirts and a pair of trousers.

A tall man suddenly walks in. "Well" Demarco, this is your patron, Mr Bannes. He'll help you get more acquainted with your new environment and give the rules to abide by. Have a good evening". The minister concludes.

I spend the rest of the evening receiving orientation about the boy's home. I was also introduced to some of them.

By the time I was done with Mr barnes. I was completely exhausted. The renewal centre sure didn't have much facilities nor equipment- a basket court and the large hall were the only social resources available. We weren't let out of the home without any tangible reason seems like a prison to me.

"Hi!" my thought is interrupted as in entered my room.

"I'm Wes!, your room mate. I'm occupying the lower bound so you gonna be my ceiling at night. I understand, I smiled at his sense of rumor "How long have you been hear?" I asked"

"Three year" He replies tying his shoes and was about to go out

"The minister and his wife received you well I guess" he speaks getting up.

"Ya!, they are nice folks"

He chuckles "They're nice on everyone's first day". H e pats my shoulders

"Welcome to hell!"

And just leaves am trying to process the last thing he said. "Wha...."

I say aloud trying to get him to come back and explain as I look back but he had already left.

"Welcome to hell?" that was something to ponder on for the night.

The next few weeks I tried to blend in making new friends. The renewal centre had boys of all ages, most younger than I was, the rest—slightly older.

The boys wore different colors of skin. Blacks were more but there were also Asians, Latinos, Caribbean, and a few Americans. The boys were previously forty-nine until I came along hanging out with Wes and some other guys at lunch break. I'm informed about the bizarre things that go on in the boy's home. Already familiar with the cult-like activities the church is involved in and weird doctrines it upheld. As the boys are being forced to go to the Baptist church every Sabbath or else punished, I wanst too surprised to hear about another evil being upheld by the minister. Still, I found it hard to digest that he was a gay pedophile taking advantages of younger boys. It was all too much to take in.

"But are you guys sure you've seen him cajole a younger kid and fuck him, or you all dwelling on rumours?" almost wishing immediately I didn't ask that question as they all shout my glares like I was stupid.

"New guy, if you don't wanna believe fine!" but remember we've been here before you and we know… Leslie goes out!

Short by Paulo "What nonsense, Leslie?" D-man, my kid brother got screwed by that son of a bitch. He came to me crying, it aint no myth. He fucks boys".

Pauolo persiste trying to drive in his point that his voice starts to go over the edge.

"shhh", quietly paolo. You don't wanna be the next Justin Clarkson". Eric tries to soothe

"Who's that?" My ignorant ass asks another question.

"He was one of us really young Justin was severely raped by the pastor. He hid his anger and hate for long, trying to bear the pain but the trauma refused to go. "

At a point I couldn't keep it no more. He just lost it. He attacked the man and was viciously beaten by those body guards. He suddenly disappeared and the only thing we heard about him was that he sent an audio to the press, explaining his action as due to the influence of heroine and that he had left the renewal home to bury his shame elsewhere no wanting to cause more trouble for the kind pastor. But we all knew that was such bullshit. We heard the audio. Fine, it was Justin but that dude would never have said that in his right senses. The media can buy that not me. As far as I am concerned, he was threatened, probably tortured to say so and later killed". Wes gulps down a glass of water.

I'm suddenly regretting coming here".

It came out so easy..

"Well now you said it, if you don't mind my asking-what prompt you into accepting that offer?" Leslie asks

"I had no choice. Life left me with none, couldn't we just run away from here?"

Everyone bows their head trying to avoid the question. "Why is everyone suddenly mute?" its easy—I say.

They let us go out, "You are not even the 10th person to conceive that thought." We all have tried to get away but we always come back

Says Eric!

"Ok, now you lost me", I reply puzzled.

They always find us before we go that far"

"How is that possible?" after a long silence, Wes finally says

"GPS"

"what the....GPS!" I screamed out mistakenly alarmed by what I just heard.

"Shush it. I'm not completely sure. It's just a hypothesis going viral. It's the only logical explanation for why we keep getting caught"

"This is jail time, so one doesn't leave here?" I ask

"when you've reached twenty, he lets you go"

"so we all still fold our arms still getting screwed, waiting for twenty?"

No one replies.

"I wish I had that patient" I mutter" but as time goes on, I had put aside every though of escaping. I was angry at everything. The shitty meals, restricted freedom, poor healt facilities and the unexplainable practices we involved in on Sabbath days. But I stayed out for too long once and they came to pick me up exactly where I was thinking I was lost since I still wasn't used to Lippincott street. So running away for now was no option. Where would I even go?. I loved the city of Flint but I needed to change location. Things were pretty messed up here. I heard once you turned twenty and wished to go you were allotted a certain amount to got start a new life. Maybe I would wait for that cash.

As I looked out the window, I sight the minster entering his newest brand new jeep with escorts following behind.

"Ass hole" I muttered

The bastard persuaded me to come so as to increase his pocket. While giving the statistics the state of Michigan would also have to fund one more person—me .

This guy collects our paycheaks and doesn't do much with it. He squandered the money on himself leaving boys home in squalor

We weren't properly equipped neither with skills nor given the education the state payed for

Its been long I got stoned. I'll follow the guys out tonight; I heard there's a new club just down the street.

By evening Wes and the others were about leaving when I tagged along. We lied about our destination and were given the pass when we got back from the club, it was almost 10pm. Its fucked up leaving a club by 10 because of a stupid rule. It was just too early. The fun was just staring. We all retired to bed, to our various rooms, quite drunk

June 2014, I had spent two years in the renewal home and I still didn't feel renewed. Maybe not completely, two full years as I'd had to to junenile prison twice for assault. First on a fellow guy in the home and second on one of the security officers at the gate. I didn't stand a chance in the latter as I was quickly encircled and beaten before put to jail. Of course, the minister had to grant me bail. He would do anything to protect his public image. I was hoping by my second crime, he would be fed-up and release me to the outside world, but I was wrong. The only thing he released was a threat.

I found myself back in the renewal centre has it has not increased much from how it was the last two years. As 20 years old were being let to go every year, with what I called "bribes" to keep them from disclosing to the public, sick shit that's been going on here, new boys also came along. But the number was few. Rumors about the minister's cult like church had already spread far in flint, alongside the news that he was a guy pedophile.

Homeless kids who of course heard this, would rather live the rest of their lives in jail than to be here. This explains why there were only eight boys who newly became part of the renewal home. They are all kids and fucked. That man can't come near me except he wanted to be beaten. I wasn't frail neither a goddamn fag. He was intimidating with his wealth and status, and I was intimidating with my face, size and .....Just then my thoughts are interrupted by a noise I freeze to listen to.

As I was about to continue to bounce the small tennis ball in my hand against the ceiling while still laying on my bunk, I stopped again to examine the ball.

Paulo

Poor Paulo

I had promised myself to visit him in prison once I got out of here.... And the others too. His kid bro, Kendrick, was gone and so was he too. Kendrick who was once molested by the highly-acclaimed minister, suddenly took ill the previous month and died. There was a sudden and high spike found in his blood. The medics argued that it shouldn't have killed him, it wasn't so effective a poison, Paulo was persistent in his own opinion that it wasn't the water.

April this year, flint changed its water supply which was from Detriot, to the river flint. The city was economically down and needed to save money. One of the means it came up with was to change the water supply thence to flint residents from the river flint. It was a disaster as the water wasn't filtered, and lead from the old pipes contaminated it making it unsafe for use. Its reported to have a long-lasting effect on children's brain and nervous system. when this was immediately learnt of some celebrities and influential church members donated stacks and stacks of packaged bottled water to the renewal center. None of which did minister Frank let us know about until recently when rumors from those who worked at the mansion started going viral about the stacks of bottled water in his house. The man wasn't only stingy but knew how to deprive others of their rights. His pet dog bathed bottled water while we left without any option but to drink lead water and eat our food cooked with poison.

Paulo, who had until then shut himself against the rest of the world, refusing to hang out with anyone and constantly blaming himself about everything that happened to Kendrick—not defending him, suddenly was bent on causing trouble for the pastor. He started a revolution that was fueled by us- his friends

Together we all staged a protest against the poor health care, bad food and water. Our protest was perceived wrongly as defiant act of violence wrongly as defiant act of violence, most of us were beaten. From the on we knew the minister wasn't someone to reason with. A stubborn, he-goat bent on oppressing others. Paulo was arrested as the leader of the protest. He was locked up ever since, he wasn't even given a trial. The minister wont want to take that risk so as not to expose his evil deeds by the confessions of a lad. I'm not sure he will be released out of prison anytime soon

"Why don't they just die?" I'm interrupted by Wes whom I wrongly assumed was asleep in the lower bunk.

They are just stubborn I guess. That is why we have to kill them

"Ya", I know.

Still I just wish they could make things easier for us. The man gat cancer and his wife also gat diabetes"

I chuckle "Wishes" don't come through"

"we going to the club this evening. You coming?" he changes the subject.

"Hell yeah, bro! count me in"

At the club that evening, I catch a glimpse of someone I'd only seen once and in a long time. I still did not know her name.

I wonder what she's doing here at Lippincott. I pushed my way through to where she is just as she's about walking away

"Uh..uhh..hi," I force out

"can I help you with something?" she asks non-chalantly sapping my courage

"I.....I...Uhm...my name is Dermaco", I pause unsure what to say next

She gives me the "who-cares?" looks and says, "well Demarco or whatever your name is, are you a stammer?"

I'm taken a little bit a back by her rude manners "We! No...No..but.."

"Then obviously your mum didn't send you to school"

Before I could hold myself back. My palm came in contact with her chubby cheeks. I was now a mad man, shaking furiously. There was no time to think, just do. Before she recovers from the shock of the slap, I grab a bottle and smashed it on her head. She screams out very loud finally drawing attention. I hold her neck tightly and pin her to the wall raising her up in the process. I did not care who it was but no one talks about mu mother that way.

Suddenly, I'm gripped and thrown to the ground. I got severely beaten and thrown in prison. "Obviously, the girl I beat is a spoilt brat who had never been to a spoilt brat who had never been to a real party all her life else she would know how to address a dude properly"

I tell myself

That was quite true as the girl's parent detained me, refusing to drop the case. I was to be charged with attempted murder.

The minister intervenes on my behalf after spending two weeks in prison. He pacifies the parents of the girl, whose name happened to be Tania. I am later released with the condition that I get a psychologist or counselor.

Tania told me a lot about her life before being here>> "flash back!"

Grrrrrrr! Grrrrrr!

The alarm buzzed. Tania hated the fact that she'd have to stand up on her feet to hit the snooze button every time the alarm went buzzing, coupled with the fact that the alarm clock was on her stereo set at a distance which seemed to be like a thousand miles away, or so she thought. In as much as she'd have loved sleep some more, she couldn't dare because she knew what comeuppance would be meted out to her. *My boss isn't that nice*, she thought

Grrrrrrr! Grrrrrr!

She woke up grudgingly, mumbling some curses under her breath as she walked to the stereo and switched off the alarm clock. *Fridays are really supposed to be free days. Why can't we just add her to the weekends already? Seriously, Saturdays and Sundays aren't just enough to compensate for the stress we go through over the weekends. It's unfair!* she thought

She sauntered towards the drapery and parted it as rays of light seeped through the room with a laser-like focus, opened the door to the balcony. She liked what she saw, it was a beautiful morning as the sun had just woken up from its slumber and now shining over the horizon, cars snaking through the traffic, kids trying to walk over the zebra crossing .It was a beautiful sight to behold

She went back into my room, just in time to see what mess she'd gotten herself into the previous night. There were shards of glass on the mahogany hardwood flooring. The room reeked of alcohol. She had had a slumber night with a close friend and confidante, Sofia the previous night. Sofia had been having problems with her relationships lately; her boyfriend, Juan had stopped giving her his attention and when she confronted him about it, he got mad about it, acted up and asked for a cool off. The turnout of event has gotten Sofia sober, she had no one else to relay her problems to other than Tania. She had brought a bottle of McDowell along for the night. And Tania, not being much of an alcoholic, got stoned and dozed off after some shots. Sofia had left in the wee hours of the morning before she woke up. She'd been good friends with Sofia for years. They met during her sophomore year at the college, and they have good friends ever since. Sofia is petite and tan-skinned with her long dark curly and wavy hair making up for her freckled face. She's like an epitome of a runway model. Her dad, a Puerto Rican engineer works off shore at one of those oil drilling companies in Qatar, and her mom is an English pharmacist who had died the previous year in an automobile accident.

She glanced at her wall clock. 7:13am! A wave of panic surged through Tania's body as she realized what time of the day it was. She knew there was no way she'd be able to beat the traffic and make it to her place of work in time because her office was like a thirty minutes' drive. And to think of the query she might receive from her boss for being, she'd better start peeing in her pant now.

She quickly grabbed her towel and ran towards the bathroom...

.

.

.

.

.

"8:45am!" she muttered as she glanced at the digital clock hung by the doorway as shetook a stride past the reception hallway. She was then greeted by lots of smugly faces; her colleagues. They all looked happy, with a smirk on their faces as some of them were just settling down officially for the day. she greeted and smiled back at that them.

As shewas about make a right turn to her cubicle, she immediately stopped in her tracks, she felt parched in her throat. She could swear she needed some water to quench her thirst at that moment. Standing at the entrance to her cubicle was her boss, a short man with a pot-belly. He looked furious at her

"Good morning sir", she said with trepidation all over her

"What's so good about the morning!" he bellowed. His voice sounding like the peal of a thunder

"I'm sorry I came late, sir. I had a long night", she stammered just to save face. Not that it was that necessary

"I'm not really interested in what you have to say. Just get me the necessary documents for today. Today is the deadline Hardman Plc. set for us. We need to get started right away and close the deal as soon as possible", he said with scowl.

"Yes sir", she replied as he left, briskly walking past her in quick pace. She caught a whiff of his perfume just in time.

"Bleu De Chanel", she muttered as I smirked

"Now!" he bellowed at some distance away

She jerked as she made motion to get into her cubicle. She had obviously forgotten that her boss has a keen sense of hearing.

It was hectic and long day at work as workers were already rounding up. Outside the building complex, the traffic was already congesting. Tania was glad she'd done all that was required of her and was just about leaving the office when her

"Oh yes!"

"Liar! Move over", Lola gestured as she sat on the hammock close to Tania's.

"I've missed you", Tania said as they both cheek kissed and the following conversation ensued.

"So how have you been?" Tania asked

"Never felt better…walking on sunshine. And you, it's been a while. I hardly get to see you these days. I guess you've been so busy" Lola smirked

Tania smiled "you and i know that that's not true. Besides I've been thinking of making that big move in my career path right now"

"Huh… there she goes again", Lola sighed

Tania snarled and gave her a nudge. Lola chuckled. "My passion for politics is waxing stronger day by day. I can't even think straight anymore. I dream about it day and night. I just feel this need to go out there and serve the people, working for the community. It's like the universe calling me to a higher purpose which is far greater than me"

"Hmmm…speaking of which, that is why I called you over. I have good news for you", Lola smiled sheepishly

Tania's eyes glowed expectantly ;as she readjusted her body position on the hammock. Lola let out a loud chuckle. Tania frowned "tell me now or I beat you up". Lola laughed "okay okay...I'll tell you."

"Well, the first good news is that..." she paused, stared intently at Tania and grinned

"Stop teasing!" Tania screamed. Lola laughed some more. "Alright then, concerning your career path, I'm already in talks with a politician who happens to be a family friend. He has promised to get back to me soon enough".

"Are you for real?"

"Oh yes! Matter of fact, when your chances of getting fixed is way high" Tania explained.

Tania let out a short, but sharp squeal, much to the hearing of everyone around her. All eyes focused in their direction. "Geez" she said as she cowered. Lola withdrew her hand after trying to close her friend's mouth with her palm. They both chuckled.

"Good gracious! That's some good news", Tania said

"Yeah baby"..."and the other good news is...", Lola added

Tania stared intently at her friend as though she was trying to see through her mind & soul; unraveling every secret therein.

"Tell me please"

"Well, my fiancé and I are walking down the aisle soon", she beamed with a smile.

"Tania paused for some seconds as though she was trying to let the whole thing sink in, and then she screamed so loud that she almost caused a stir; disturbing the magical ambience in the garden. There was a murmur in the garden. Lola chuckled.

"Wow! I'm happy for you, sweetheart!", Tania exclaimed as she hugged Lola tight

"Thank you so much baby"

"Wow, this call for some celebration"

"Naah. Not tonight darling. I need to go to bed early tonight as I have an appointment tomorrow morning with my dentist. But –"she quickly added". I promised to make it up to you next time"

"That's okay…oh my gosh, am so happy for you". Tania said with gleefulness

They discussed about some other things for some minutes, then bade each other goodnight

Later that night, Tania was in her apartment, she had just taken her bath. Dressed in her pajamas, she was on her sofa, checking and replying her mails. She was just about to retire for the night when her phone beeped. She smiled.

Hello baby", the sexy baritone voice echoed over the line.

"Hi Sweetie", Tania smiled. It was Mike, her college sweetheart. They'd been dating even after college and when he got a job as a sales marketer. Things were cool a couple of months until he was transferred to head the Marketing Department of one of the company's firm in Singapore. Ever since then, their relationship had been lukewarm sort of; no sparks, no glitz, just embers of what was once a beautiful and flawless relationship. They still got in touch from time to time though, but it wasn't as what it used to be.

"How are you, flawless?"

"I'm fine darling. I hope you're doing well"

"Yeah... i am"

"I miss you"

"I do too, baby"

"I wish you were here with me"

She purred "I could say the same here too, honey"

They kept talking for some minutes as they tried to catch up on old times; the reminiscence of the funny times made them both to laugh. He hung up after a while; she smiled as she crept up to her bed.

That was the inscription on a life-sized portrait of Abraham Lincoln that was hung on the wall in the lounge of the office building. The air smelled of rose and lavender. Lola had called Tania three days earlier after they had met at their favorite relaxation spot. She had told her that the politician who happens to be the Alderman of the country had agreed to the request and that he had scheduled a one-on-one interview with her. Tania was so happy that she couldn't wait for this D-day. On this Tuesday morning, she had had her colleagues cover up for her at her place of work. Also, she had switched off her mobile phone so her boss' call wouldn't come through. Dressed up to the nines, she had walked into this sprawling office complex where the meeting had been arranged. Lola had sent her the address earlier that morning. And before she left her apartment, she had proposed in her mind that she was going to comport herself in the most appropriate professional poise, answering virtually all the questions that he would ask in a cool, calm and collective manner.*He's gonna like me*, she thought

"Good morning, how may I help you?" the receptionist asked her, looking at the beautiful face for the fraction of a second before going back to what she was typing.

"Good morning, ma'am, I have an appointment with the Alderman, Dr. Cole" Tania reeled off the words. The receptionist stopped typing abruptly and stared at her for a millisecond. "What's the name if I may -?"

"Tania Jones", she interrupted

"Hold on for a minute", she said, touch typing on her computer screen.

I'm sorry but you have no appointment with the Alderman today" she said almost without looking at svelte figure standing across her hand-carved oak desk. "But-" she quickly added, "let me put a call through"

"Thanks", Tania said, shaking her finger sin reflex. She was becoming nervous; probably due to the fact that she was already having a premonition that she was going to be disappointed. But she had practiced meditation earlier that morning; how could her mind play peekaboo on her at this very crucial moment of her life. *Stop acting funny!*She chided herself

"Who referred you to him?" the receptionist interrupted her thoughts

"Lola… Lola Balogun" she quickly added.

The receptionist nodded, and then said something inaudible. She hung up almost immediately. "The secretary asked me to let you in. The office is by the right wing, first floor."

Good heavens, Tania muttered as she made motion towards the elevator.

"Use the staircase please. We're having technical issues with the elevator today" the receptionist quickly added

"Oh alright", Tania said she made a swift turn to the left towards the staircase.

When she got to the alderman's office, she met an elderly woman with blonde hair, who appeared to be in her late forties sitting on the desk. *That must be secretary,* she thought

"Good morning" Tania greeted

"Good morning. The alderman has been expecting you. But he's in a meeting at the moment. Have a seat please"

"Thanks", Tania sat as she made motion to sit down on a divan adjacent to the secretary's desk.

Two minutes later, two men walked out of the alderman's office; a black man and a Latino. The black guy who dressed corporately in an Armani suit held a briefcase while the Latino dressed casually. They greeted the secretary as they were about to leave. The Latino glanced at Tania for like a second or two, and then he kept a straight face as they both walked briskly; out of sight. He looked familiar somehow. She could have sworn that she knew him from somewhere. *That's not the reason why I'm here'*, she quickly reminded herself.

It was barely a minute when the alderman called the secretary.

"Alright sir" *Beep* .She hung up "You can go in now"

"Thank you very much, madam"

The madam looked at Tania and frowned "you're welcome". Tania noticed her sudden countenance and quickly faced the direction with which was going to. At the door, the placard read "OFFICE OF THE 2nd ALDERMAN; MR. CURTIS WILLIAMS".

Tania paused for a second, and then drew a long breath.

"Come on in", the voice called

She shuddered, readjusted her tousled shirt and opened the door.

There he was, a fine gentleman who appeared to be in his early forties. He was just taking off his tweed jacket, his torso and abs looked well-toned as revealed in the shirt he wore. He was fumbling for some files on the shelf when Tania had entered

"Good morning sir", Tania managed to greet

"Good morning. Have a seat", he answered

Tania sat down on the swivel chair that was positioned in front of his hand-crafted oak desk. The desk looked like a replica of the one she saw at the receptionist's stand.

"Lola talked about you having a passion for politics", the Alderman said as he kept a dull face, with one hand on his chin. He looked forlorn.

"Yes sir", Tania said as she tried to fumble for words that didn't come right through. She gave him her CV. He flipped through the pages. "SoMiss Tania Jones…" he paused, staring at her ring finger. Tania smiled

"Tell me about you"

"Well, I'm Tania Jones, a graduate of History and International Relations-", she reeled off her resume.

"Okay. So why politics? Why the drive for it?" the Alderman questioned Tania. She sat upright and took a deep breath "well sir, it's a passion for me. Right from my school days, I've always found myself participating in groups, holding the leadership position, always being the one assigned to hold responsibility and conduct due to my relentless effort in making sure that everything works out. I'm an organizer and a decision-maker; I always find myself wanting to do more for people, not for my own selfish interest. I love to serve, I love to lead, and I believe feel I can achieve my goals here; working for the people of the community"

The Alderman mused, staring at Tania for a while. He asked her about few more questions to which Tania answered modestly

"So what's your relationship with Lola?" he asked

Tania relaxed "Lola and I have been childhood friends for as far as I can remember. We are more of family friends, as our parents are friends to each other too. We used to be together on holidays. However, her parents relocated to Nigeria as at one time like that. Wanting her to complete her education here, her uncle in Compton took her into custody. We lost contact for years until I ran into her during my freshman year. We became close friends ever since then, sharing good and old times"

The Alderman kept mute for some seconds. "Alright, you can go now"

Tania was puzzled, just like that? *Did I impress him enough?* *So what happens now?* She kept thinking as she was rose up to her feet.

"You can get your appointment letter from the Secretary. Your work starts tomorrow. And no late coming please. Have a good day", the Alderman said while drafting on a piece of paper.

"oh my gosh!" Tania exclaimed. "Thank you very much sir"

The Alderman sighed and waved her off "Yeah yeah, you can go now".

Tania got the appointment letter from the Secretary and went home in high spirit. She resigned the following day, much to the bewilderment of her colleagues and boss. "You of all people should know that you are one of the best workers we have in this firm. Why would you want to resign at a time such as this?"her boss had said, butshe explained why she wanted to leave. She was wished well by her colleagues; some of them hugging her while some waved at her just as she was about leaving. She felt sickening rush of nostalgia all over her as she drove off.

About a month later, having learnt the nitty-gritty of what her job entailed, Tania had so blended into the system of the office that it seemed as though she had been there all along.. She was polite to everyone that had come her way without being so hypocritical about it. She was loved by all as she was so natural in all her doings around the office.

"Hi. Can i get a spare CD from you? I've exhausted the ones I have", Tania asked Sarah, the secretary

Sarah took a CD and handed it over to Tania "here you go darling", she said

"Thank you, Mrs. Tanning", Tania said but was cut short

"Wait. Hold up, young lady", she said. "The next time you call me madam or Mrs. or what have you, we're going have some problem." she snapped at her

Tania nodded with a smile.

"My name is Sarah please, thank you", she said with a smirk at the corner of her mouth

"Alright... Sarah?" Tania said as struggling to pronounce the name. She nodded in the affirmative and winked at Tania. Tania chuckled and left

During the downtime at the office, Sarah was just about leaving her office adjacent to Curtis' when she met the Secretary looking despondent. She didn't even notice Tania was there

"Hello Sarah" she greeted

No response

"Sarah..." she greeted again; her voice was louder this time around

Sarah jerked. "Oh my God! You just freaked me out"

"Sorry I didn't mean to", Tania said.

She sat upright "So what's up?"

"Wanna grab some lunch?" Tania asked

She sighed "No I think I'll pass" she said. She stared at Tania for a while "you seem to enjoy what you do"

Tania squinted "really? What is it that I do?"

"Making other people happy and comfortable with you, going about your work with much gusto and all", Sarah added

Tania smiled "happiness is from inside out. You can't give to people what you don't have"

"You know, I've always wondered how you still manage to do all that despite the fact we've been going through some shakedown in the office lately. You seem not to be perturbed".

Tania smiled. Sarah continued "You know I didn't like you at first. You seemed to exude this aura of love that I haven't had for a while and -" she paused, musing as though she felt she had committed some Freudian slip there

Tania, being the kind of person she is had understood that there was a missing loop there. Ordinarily, she would have skipped that part of the conversation and drift it to something else. But no, she felt she needed to know what was bothering Sarah. She smiled, and sat down on Sarah's oak desk.

"So tell me about you Sarah, I've actually grown fond of you over the few weeks that I've known you,and I'd love to know you more" Tania smiled as she asked her, crossing her arms in akimbo

Sarah paused for a while… stared at her ring finger and sighed. "Most people don't really know much about me in the office because I'm always trying to mind my business.i don't stick up my nose in where it doesn't belong"

Tania nodded so as to urge her on

"I just got divorced some months back and right now, it seems like my whole world is falling apart. My relationship with my husband was heading towards the rock so we had to call it quit…went through 17 years of hell with that bastard. It wasn't a nice experience. He was a liar, a cheat and a drunk. I thought I could change him but over the years, I realized…that letting go of the hurt, the past and the negativity that tags along with it is always better than holding on"

She looked at Tania. She seemed engrossed in her sob story. So she continued "I had a psychopathic crack head for a son. He passed away some years ago", she sobered

"Oh no…I'm so sorry Sarah", Tania apologized

"No you don't have to be, dear". She added "Now I'm all about to finding love again…after 21 years, can anybody ever love me again? "She said with trickles of tears cascading down her cheeks

"Oh dear, don't be like that. You will. I'm sure you will". Tania said as she held Sarah's head to her chest.

"I know that you're just trying your best to console me. You see, I've been binge-eating lately as a result of the emotional stress that I've been going through, I'm aging, I'm getting fatter, I don't even have a child anymore. I've got nothing else to live for', she kept on crying

"Hush" Tania said as she tried to console her. "Don't say that. You have something else to live for"

Sarah stopped crying, freed herself from Tania's cuddling hands. Looking serious now "What else do I have to live for?" she said, wiping her face of with the back of her wrist. She seemed to wanting to listen to what Tania had to say.

Tania was caught by surprise. She didn't know what to say that would made sense to Sarah. Either ways, she had to say something sensible to cheer up. "See it is not too late to start all over again. All your problems can be gone if you want them to; if you're desperate enough to get rid of them. As for love, you'll find it. But first of all you'd have to shed off some weight and stop eating junks. You need to look sizzling"

Still staring at Tania, she continued "Look, there's this fitness gym where I do work out on weekends, I can get you signed up there. Let's start from there"

Tania paused as she saw sarcasm written on the face of Sarah. When Sarah realized she had gotten the message. She let out a deep laugh, with tears still trickling down her cheeks "Gym class? Me?" She snorted "I'd rather swim in an ocean with great white sharks"

Tania laughed and poked her in her ribcage. She cringed "I'm serious, Sarah? You can do this. Cardio workouts make you feel good about yourself"

"That is no option, girl. Talk about something better please" she kept laughing

"Alright then, but how about Yoga?" Tania asked, squinting

Sarah scrunched up her nose, thought about it for a while. "Well I think that would be better. I heard it's chilled"

"How can you even do Yoga when you can't even fully swing your body in exercise", Tania queried. "We're doing both". She ended up saying

"You don't call the shots here baby, I do" Sarah said with her mouth agape in astonishment

"No I do. Since you don't know what you want, I'll help you. It's your life, but imma get it back for you ", Tania said, rising up and walking away briskly, laughing at the bewildered secretary

"No you can't have me do that!" Sarah's voice howling from behind

"Sure I can...and I will", Tania fired back as she was just about pressing the elevator button

"No?"

"Yes"

"No!"

"And a hell yes!" Tania giggling

Beepbeep

The elevator closed and moved downwards.

Curtis was at the gas station. He had gone to visit his Dad earlier that morning in another city. They talked for a while, sharing good memories. His dad, being an ex-convict and a daredevil had advised him concerning his political career never to quit at what he felt was right and appropriate, even if it would cost him his life. He gave an example of greatest black men in the history of United States. He ended up with the words "Boy, if the cause isn't greater than your life, then it isn't worth it"

He drove for some miles into his city. Realizing that his fuel tank was displaying the warning sign, he decided to drive in to this gas station. After swiping the cards, he drove off to his office. On getting to the office, he running through some paper works when he realized that hehad forgotten one of the necessary documents at home he needed to scan and push to an email address. He left the office hurriedly, barely saying a word or two to his secretary. Quickly, he hurried into the parking lot and drove his Benz off.

About 15 minutes later, he pulled up in his garage and walked straight towards the porch, with his eyes scanning the neighborhood, nothing spectacular, just the same old place. He sighed and walked into his apartment, noticing that the door was left slightly ajar, he moved towards the living room, he heard the shower running. Maybe Quincy is having her bath. It was unusual for him to have to come back so early in the day. He didn't bother going upstairs. He went straight to the kitchen to make some toast bread. As he plugged the toaster, he heard some muffled voices. What could be happening upstairs? He thought

Switched off the toaster, he proceeded upstairs. "Hey darling", he called out

No movement. No response. What could be happening? He thought

Suddenly, his instincts kicked in. He started walking on tiptoes, almost soundlessly; straight to his wife's room. He stopped at the entrance of the door of the bedroom, the door was closed, but the shower was still running. He could have barged into the room. But he knew better. He tried to eavesdrop but the water running made it impossible to hear what was happening. He checked through the peephole

Nothing

He was just about to turn the knob and open the door when he stopped again, there was something else; he saw something that seemed to be like a silhouette on the Mahogany hardwood flooring, breezing past the living room from the kitchen

*No, not the kitchen... it's downstairs. Shit! Check the backdoor downstairs!*Instantly, Curtis ran down the staircase; some steps down, and voila!He jumped downstairs and ran towards the backdoor.

Saturday Morning, 7:45am

Sarah and Tania had just ended the Yoga meditation session and the cardio workouts. Sarah had been noticing physical changes in her body some weeks after she had signed up for a fitness and yoga class. She was so happy about it that she kept thanking Tania for pushing her through. Her BMI had reduced significantly within weeks. The happiness even reflected in her aura so much that it got people talking at the office. She used to have a phobia for aging, but the fear subsided and now, she felt young all over again. Some days ago, a handsome gentleman who looked to be in his fifties hooked her up as she went shopping for her groceries at a mall. She was elated today, giving Tania a gist of how the hook-up went and how the man had asked her out on a date. Both of them were happily having the conversation while packing up their fitness kits.

"Oh good heavens, I'm so happy for you", Tania said happily as they were about to exit the building. They crossed the tarmac to an open field where their cars were parked and made motion to sit down on a pew close by.

Later, the conversation drifted to office gossips.

"I don't know if I'm supposed to ask you this. But I'm worried. Our boss hasn't been happy lately. What could be the problem? "She questioned Sarah

Sarah mused for moment "you see, it's more than what you think it is" she said. "Mr.Curtis Williams used to be close friends to the mayor. He even used to cut the mayor's hair way back then. The mayor encouraged him to run for the position of Alderman; he even helped him at some point. But later when he won, another white alderman introduced him to the township supervisor, the mayor felt the aldermen were sitting down with the enemy and has been attacking Curtis; trying to get him out of that seat ever since" she explained

Tania thought about it for a while

"The Mayor and his loyalists have plunged this city into debts by siphoning public funds into their pockets for the past 9 years", she added

"What! Are you serious now?" Tania queried

"Ain't kidding, girl"

Sarah's phone rang. She picked the call and after she hung up. She told Tania she had to go as she had some things to do. They bade each other farewell and left.

The climate had changed over the weeks and the atmospheric condition was becoming sultry. On this particular day, Sarah and Tania had just gotten into the office after having lunch together. They continued their conversation, laughing and all. Then the mayor of the city walked in, accompanied by his aide. He had come to visit Curtis.

"Hello. Is Mr. Williams in?" he asked, keeping a straight face

"Hello Dr. Blanc" Sarah stuttered "Yes of course, you -"

He had already barged into Curtis' office without the consent of the secretary. Sarah and Sophie stared at each other in unison and then shrugged. He was the bigger boss, so there was barely anything they could do about it. They heard them trying to muffle their voices as they engaged each other in a hot argument

About thirty minutes, the mayor and his aide left, without saying a word to either Sarah or Tania.

Sarah was about to say a word to Tania when Curtis interrupted their conversation "You both should get to your work and stop gossiping" it was Curtis coming out of his office. He had his sleeves rolled up, and kept a straight face. "Sarah", he called

"Yes boss"

"i want you to help me to review my book. I just finished writing it and I want you to be the first to check it out. I want to publish it before the end of the year" he said, handing a USB stick over to Sarah

"Straight away, boss" she said, clicking her tongue. She put the stick into a USB port into her laptop and got started.

"And you Tania, I need to have a word with you" he said, walking back his office without glancing at her. Tania followed and closed the door.

He walked up to a cabinet, picked a particular file and threw it on the table, landing with a thud "I've been having challenges lately" he added "… with the powers that be" slumping on his swivel chair

"I know this is beyond the normal office conversation but I need you to ask you some sensitive questions. This shouldn't go beyond these walls, okay? I need to ask you, what do you do when you're literally fed up?"

"It would depend on what I'm actually fed up of', she answered, their eyes in contact

Curtis didn't say a word. "What could be wrong boss?" she asked him

He sighed "This shouldn't go beyond these walls", pointing at the corner wall

"Alright", Tania said, wondering what he had to say that was so classified

"Have a seat" he motioned to her. She sat down and listened intently

"I'm having issues with the mayor recently"

"Dr. Blanc?" Tania asked

"Yes I know I should have told you about this earlier, but I figured Sarah would have, based on your level of relationship with her. She trusts you".

Tania nodded

"Dr. Blanc has been having issues with me because of my relationship with the Township supervisor. He felt I was sleeping with the enemy so he tried to pay me off so I could resign, I refused. Then he tried to bribe me, I renegedat the eleventh hour. Ever since then, I've been a potential target for criticisms and law suits. Matter of fact, I've been sued twice. Just now, the mayor, through his lawyerslammed me with a fresh count charge; felony, assault and battery

"Battery?" she asked, surprised

Yeah. There was a time I had a heated argument with the mayor's aide. He was saying gibberish, I didn't know when I lost control, so I hit him.

"Wow", Tania sighed

"Yeah. I was already on the verge of resigning before you came. You changed my mindset...unknowing to you"

Tania gaped

"I don't know how to explain this but you seem to exude this positive vibe that I still don't understand... now the working atmosphere around this place has changed. You kind of made my burden lighter with the way you went about the work here. So I told myself I wasn't gonna resign anyway. Imma stay to see how this goes down."

There was a brief silence

"You should get to work. I'll send for you when I need you", he asked

"Alright then", she said and left his office

Curtis was outside his house on a cool Saturday, the air smelled sterile. He was lying stretched on his sun lounger under the shade, reading his favorite Wall Street Journal. With a cup of cappuccino on the tray near him, he was content; feeling cool. He'd had a little quarrel with his wife that morning, and she was ready for a showdown but he wasn't going to have any of it. Today isn't the day of reckoning, he had promised himself. So here was outdoor, under a tree, chilling. About thirty minutes later. A courier van drove by his house, alighting from the vehicle was a short, fat man with beard. He seemed to be having problems with wriggling his plus sized body out of the car, grunting at each every twist and turn of his body. Finally, he broke through. Curtis watched in amusement as the man dropped the mail into his mailbox. He waved at Curtis; Curtis reciprocated with a mischievous grin, the mail man then got back to his vehicle. Curtis watched in anticipation of the next drama unfolding. But surprisingly, the man got into his driver seat with ease. Curtis clasped his hands with a sigh. Game over! He had just been let down. He stood up in a bid to go retrieve the mail from the mailbox. There was a hollow blast of siren some distance far away from his residence. He read what was written on the mail, it read "U.S. Bank Home Mortgage". Curious to know what was therein, he proceeded to open and check. In an instant, his countenance changed. Without hesitating, he marched furiously into his apartment.

"Quincy! Where the hell are you?" He bellowed

"Quincy!" He marched upstairs. He barged into his bedroom, and stopped dead in his tracks. There was his wife stuffing clothes into her travelling bag. She seemed not perturbed in the least sense.

"What the fuck is this supposed to mean!" he said furiously, throwing the paper at her

She didn't even bother to read it. It was as though she'd known what was coming, and she was all ready for that showdown she didn't get earlier that morning. She kept packing her stuffs.

"Woman, answer me before I deal with -"

"Shut the fuck up, motherfucker" she interrupted

"What are you gonna do? No tell me what are you gonna do to me!!" She snarled, shouting on top of her lungs

"In this house, I pay all the bills; I do the grocery shopping, and the cooking. All you do is to sit at home all day, doing nothing. You ain't got money. Nigga you're broke as fuck. See I'm even tired of all the shit you put me through. Do you think this is how I intend to keep putting up with you for the rest of my life? No way. I'm done and over with you. You can go hell for all i care. Matter of fact, I'm leaving this minute. I now have someone who values me more than you do, I'm sure you know him already. He's gonna take care of me real good and be a better man than you ever were. Sissy good-for-nothing silly ass bitch! I'm out!" She said as she picked her bags, pushed him out of the way and hurried downstairs, her hold all wheeling behind her. For a moment, Curtis seemed to be held spellbound

"I...i don't understand any of this", he stammered. "Could this be because of Juan?"

She made a halt the moment she heard Curtis spilled the bean; she was already downstairs by this time. And for a moment or two, she made up her mind, turned back and faced him. Her countenance was fiery

"Yes! You can say that over and over again. I thought you were a better man but he proved otherwise. So for that, I'm sticking with him." she snarled and made towards the door.

"So...baby, what am I supposed to do now that you're leaving?" Curtis said, with tears streaming down his face

"I DON'T CARE!! And you know what? I wish you hell in this world and beyond!", she thundered, opened the door and tried to wriggle out her bag

"Quincy!" He shouted

She stared back at him in annoyance

"Baby please, what about our son, please consider" he pleaded

"You go fuck yourself!" She interrupted as she banged the door. Hard!

With his back against the wall, he gradually slumped until he sat down on the hardwood flooring with a soft thud, he thought about how frustrating his life was going to be without his wife. He thought about his son Gabby in jail and the Mayor trying to soil his name in the mud. It was as though the whole world was against him

Some seconds later, he could hear the engine of her car revving up, and in a moment, the car sped off. Lying spread-eagled with his back against the mahogany hardwood flooring, he wailed uncontrollably, hitting his fists on the floor each time his emotions got to the peak.

After a long while, he slept there on the floor in no time as the soft breeze breezing through the window near him kept caressing his face.

It was on a sunny afternoon as Tania walked into this Mexico café that Curtis had arranged to meet her at. She squinted as she tried to scan through the whole lounge for him. There he was, looking casual. He wore a plain blue T-shirt on a pair of jeans. With *his* hands rested on his laps, he kept tapping his fingers nervously. He looked tired and forlorn. As his eyes were busy scanning through the area, he caught the sight of his personal assistant. His eyes glowed instantly. Tania smiled as she witnessed the sudden transformation of his countenance. Wow, she thought

"Hey" he greeted nervously, his finger still tapping his thighs as Tania got to the table. He readjusted his sitting position

"Hi", Tania replied, looking into his eyes

"Have a seat", he said uneasily

"How have you been, boss?" Tania asked

"I haven't been okay, really"

Tania smiled and held his right palm. He was wearing Michael Korrs wristwatch. He looked into her eyes "thanks for coming", he said, with his eyes clouded.

There was a brief silence save for other people talking in hush tones and cutlery clinking.

"My apartment is going to be foreclosed this week"

"What? Why?" Tania puzzled

"I got a mail stating that I haven't been paying my mortgages and that I'm being evicted"

"But I thought you and your wife talked about it!" She exclaimed

"Quincy hadn't been paying all along. Now she's filing a divorce suit"

"What!" Tania bewildered

Curtis raised his hands up and smacked them on his laps "I'm fed up". "Her boyfriend also rammed into my car and totaled it recently. That was a clear message from her; someone I lived with for like 20 years. I forgave her boyfriend, but not until after I whooped his ass" he added, pounding his tight fists on his thighs.

"Oh dear!" Tania exclaimed

"she had told me that she was gonna see to it that I ended up miserable and now I'm homeless, not getting paychecks, i don't have a car and my son is in jail. What have I done to deserve all these", Curtis sighed

After what seemed to be a minute of silence, Tania spoke up

"Sorry about that" she apologized, patting him on his left thigh

"It's okay" he said as he leaned backwards

"Ehm... Since I have a spare car, i was thinking if you could have it for now", Tania managed to say

"What? Oh no, you don't need to do that", Curtis said

"C'mon, it's what friends do for each other", Tania said

Silence

Please? Tania pleaded, battling her eyelashes

Curtis laughed. "Thank you for your kind gesture. I really appreciate"

Tania smiled. "Hey bro" Curtis called out to one of the ushers waiting tables, "could you help me get a glass of sunset Margarita please? Thank you" he said politely like a gentleman. Tania phone pinged, a mail came through. She checked the message. "What would you like to drink?" Curtis interrupted her thoughts as she was typing on her phone.

Tania raised her head up slowly noticing the waiter for the first *time "Para beber, quiero el vino blanco. Gracias"* she told the waiter with a smile. The waiter left

"Wow", Curtis said, looking away

"I know right", Tania grinned

"I never knew you could speak Spanish", Curtis said, staring at her fingernails.

She yawned, making use of her handkerchief "Well it's not like I'm that perfect. I have a Puerto Rican girlfriend who taught me a wee bit of the Spanish basics." She said, swiping the screen of her phone quickly

"You've never told me you have another friend apart from Lola", he grinned

She laughed "we used to be close friends way back then in school; Lola, Sofia and i" she said showing him a picture of Sofia with a guy. "That's my crazy friend there" she grinned

Curtis stared at the picture for a while, then his eyes shone in disbelief "who's this guy next to Sofia?" He asked

Tania shrugged "her boyfriend?"

"This is Quincy's boyfriend!' "He exclaimed, trying to bring out his phone from his pocket. He scrolled through his gallery and showed her a picture. Tania's mouth was agape the moment she saw the picture.

"Remember the guy that almost choked you to death after I dropped you off that night? Remember he used a guitar string on you" He reminded her

"Yes?" Tania said, leaning forward

"Quincy's boyfriend is a music and dance instructor. That's what he does for a living", he concluded

Tania thought about it for a while "Yes, Sofia told me about how romantic he could be when he sings to her with a flamenco guitar. I think she made mention of him being a music instructor too"

Curtis clapped once "the jig is up!" exclaimed

"Curtis...Curtis "Tania said slowly, tapping him; her mouth agape, looking beyond the transparent fiberglass window

"Yeah, what's wrong?" he asked as he tried to look in the direction her eyes were;

A few distances across the café, a Cherokee Jeep that had been parked there for a while started its ignition, skidded and sped off.

It was 4:26pm. Tania wanted to brief her boss about the meeting that was to be held in a conference center the following day. When she opened the door, she saw her boss on his swivel chair, with arms folded on the desk supporting his head as he laid it to rest. He seemed to be having a nap time. She could have thought so at least, but the bottle of Ciroc and a tot glass which was half empty said otherwise

"Hello boss" Tania managed to say

"Hey...come on in" Curtis responded with apathy

"What's going on?" Tania asked, concerned about the state in which she met him

This time, he raised his head up and fell back on the backrest of the chair with a dull thud. "I'm literally fed up" he said, raising his hands up and smacking his palms on the arms of the chair in exasperation.

Tania observed his reaction for a while. "Boss I was thinking we could take some time off so we could talk about this. I know a place that's so serene; you'll love there"

He whimpered for some seconds, and then with almost no warning, he stood up with much gusto, fumbled for his car keys and phone. "Let's go", he said without looking at her face

Twenty three minutes later, they were at a private beach. The sun which had already turned orange was setting while playing peekaboo in the high clouds. Everywhere was calm and serene, save for the splashing sound of the ocean tides on the rocks. The fine pebbles and shells dotted the wealth of sands on which the tall palm trees were, swaying in the cool breeze. The incredible blue ocean surrounding this beach stretched away to the horizons. Curtis and Lola were lying side by side on the hammock that was tied between two palms trees. The cool effect of the breeze seemed to have had impact on him as he was noticeably less disturbed unlike when we were in the office. They were both talking about the funny things that had been happening. Curtis seemed to be the one cracking the jokes while Lola kept laughing hard.

"I never knew you were this hilarious really", Tania said in between the laughs

"Really? So you think I'm just a programmed robot who's only concerned with having the office job done and all?" Curtis queried " Naah, I've gotta have some fun too baby" ..."I'm a human too", he quickly chipped in

Tania laughed hard. She started coughing after that. "Take care, don't die here girl. Ain't got money for medical bills "Curtis said, jokingly

Tania gave him a nudge with her elbows "Ouch that hurts", he groaned

"Sorry", Tania giggled

There was a moment of insufferable silence. The sound of the ocean tides could still be heard from a distance far away. Some couples were close to the beach, throwing pebbles into the ocean. Overhead, some birds were flying; the palm trees seemed to be having a good time today. Indeed, nature is bliss. Curtis and Tania were still on the hammock, each thinking of what to say to the other. Curtis finally broke the silence.

"Hey" he said, his voice cracked, filled with nostalgia of some sort

Tania casted her glance on him "Thank you" he said, looking grateful

Tania purred, looking into his starry eyes

"You know...I've been faced with much trials and tribulations over the past few months that I never for once thought that I'd breakthrough. I'd always thought that I'd end up broken with some psycho-neurotic disease, or maybe I'll just die anyway as a result of the overwhelming emotional stress. But -" he added," but then, just out of the blues...you came", Curtis said passionately

Tania felt her eyes swollen with tears. But she didn't want make it so obvious, so she suppressed the urge to sob.

"I used to have this kind of relationship with Lola way back then" he continued. "Before I contested for the seat..."looking at Tania, he realized she was all smiles. He fired on "I actually happen to know her parents. We were so close. But things being the way they were, there was nothing I could do about it. I was married already and i don't cheat. After a while, the level of the closeness dwindled as my wife got a wind of it. She got the message and moved on, I also did. And now that my relationship is finally hitting the iceberg, she's about to taking hers to a new level with another guy" he sighed. "It's a cruel twist of fate" he added, raising his hands and placing it on his forehead.

There was a silence for a minute or so. Then Tania spoke up

"Was that why you gave me an appointment straight away?" She asked

He paused. "I couldn't have refused her. And I knew that for her to have referred you to me, you must then be good at that you do."

"Actually, I've worked with some politicians in the past. But it didn't work out in the end. They were being shady in their dealings; changing figures. I couldn't put up with that and so I had to resign"

"Oh really, but you didn't tell me that", Curtis said

"Yes I didn't. I was scared of saying that because I felt it could hinder my chances of getting of the job"

Curtis mused "It doesn't matter...you're here now. And thank God I did...'cause to me, you're like a blessing in disguise" he chipped in

Tania felt a fresh welling of tears trickling down her face, to her ears and hair. She felt like hugging him tight. She had never felt that way in a long while. "Thanks boss, it's an honour to work for -"

"Call me Curtis" he interrupted, looking at her in the face this time around, her face so close to his

For a moment, I thought something magical was going to happen.

"It's late already. Let's go home" Curtis said, checking his phone

He helped Tania off the hammock. They left the beach, after checking out. The security men at the gate of the beach waved at them as the Mercedes-Benz GL 500 sped off into the night, leaving trails of dust in its wake

On Tuesday morning, there were mobs outside the courthouse, holding peaceful protests. Some of their placards read "LEAVE CURTIS ALONE", "CURTIS CARES FOR THE PEOPLE", "THE ALLEGATIONS WERE NOT TRUE" and so on. Mr. Curtis Williams arrived early enough and was greeted by a throng of mobs. He waved at them and raised his hands up, observing the famous 'black power salute'. The crowd went haywire as they kept chanting his name. He walked into the courthouse together with his lawyer who was holding a conversation with him in regards to how proceeding was to go. Just last week, the mayor had filed lawsuits against him; accusing him of felony, assault and battery. The trial started on time and some hours later, the magistrate ruled the appeal in his favour; he had emerged victorious. He hugged his lawyer, Tania and everyone else around him. There was a loud ovation in the courthouse. The mobs outside were already frenzied the moment the news got to them that he had been vindicated. They kept chanting his name.

Walking with a sense of pride, he got out of the courthouse with his winning team and addressed the crowd with a great deal of enthusiasm and spirit of camaraderie.

"Fellow comrades, I greet you all. My name is Curtis Williams and I'm the second alderman of this county. Recently, I have been faced with political challenges. Some higher powers have vowed to displace me and render me useless. Why? These people siphon public treasuries into their greedy pockets. They are scared that I might blow up their cover. But y'all know what? I'm a just man, I have a great deal of integrity, I wouldn't be able to live with myself watching people suffer while i take from them that which belongs to them. I've been mauled, pushed to the wall long enough, but now I have decided to come out bold as lion and confront these thieving cabals. I am not afraid anymore; I'm like a big bone stuck in their throat, they can't do me anything. I'll keep fighting for justice for this city until I make sure that the citizens are given their due benefits. Thank you all for supporting, thank you all for standing by me. God bless you all" he ended with gusto and saluted before he got into his car. The crowd roared in frenzy as Tania drove him off with his Lawyer in the front seat

"So where are we heading to?" he asked

"To the city hall, I arranged for a press briefing on your behalf

Why? I thought we was going to the office to celebrate

"You need to understand. Your name was soiled for the wrong reason, but you were vindicated thankfully. At this point, the mayor and his loyalists are vulnerable so it is only wise for you to come out and attack them openly and verbally now that the odds are in your favour. "His Lawyer reeled out the words effortlessly.

"So what happens now?" Curtis asked

"You know what you have to do when you get in there. That's an offensive but yet effective strategy of winning this; once and for all", his Lawyer said

Curtis mused for a while "Alright then"

"Game?" his Lawyer asked

Curtis sighed "Yeah…game" as they bumped their fists.

Some minutes later, Curtis was already seated with a lots of microphones positioned in front of him, the cameramen where already taking shots and the press conference began.

"Can we meet you sir?" one of the journalists voiced out

Curtis began "thank you. I'm Curtis Williams, the 2nd Alderman of this county. It is an honour and privilege for me to be sitting in front of you all today. You see, I had a tough childhood, living in a neighborhood that was a hub of gangsters, junkies and psychos. I grew up knowing that my dad; a daredevil was a crack addict who spent most of his adult years in jail. I never knew my mom and so, I didn't grow up with the motherly love. It was really tough i tell you. Now, growing up that way, I went from being a product of these things over the years to actually moving forward to becoming a success. Now, some people wondered how I was able to do that. It was simple; I had to change my mind-set. I knew I couldn't live that way; letting myself to be a victim of circumstances. I actually moved from being a victim to being a victor. And today, I give thanks to God who made it possible for me to become one of the aldermen of the city council. It wasn't by chance or effort, it was and has still been God's grace all through

The crowd roared in applause

Another journalist asked him "sir, you've been charged with so many offences lately. Do you feel this speaks well of you as a credible alderman?"

Curtis didn't waste time "Recently I've been faced with so many charges count against me. And as you all know, I just got back from the court trial where I emerged as the victor for the third time; vindicating me of all the charges. In as much as I wouldn't like to call names, I feel it is expedient to tell you all what has been happening behind the propaganda. The mayor, with the help of other greedy aldermen has been looting this city dry for the past 9 years until I came. And when I refused to join their clique, they decided to take me out by creating some strategic distractions; misusing the taxpayer's money in an attempt to insult me instead of taking care of the city business, filing lawsuits against me, thereby soiling my reputation." Over the past few months, the Dr. Blanc has spent hours during the city council meetings talking about me and my loyalists, instead of finding solutions to the problems that is plaguing this city for a good nine years. This city suffers from high levels of poverty, unemployment and high levels of crime with run down homes, dilapidated buildings. He should be held responsible for all these…"

Curtis was asked some other questions to which he answered perfectly. The press conference ended up with a clapping ovation as Curtis and his team left the hall.

He shook hands with his lawyer, thanking him for the day as they both parted ways. Tania had offered to drive him, but he insisted he drove her home.

Thirty minutes later, Curtis pulled up in the front of her apartment. She bade him goodnight and was about to leave when Curtis held her hands in a firm, but yet soft way. She turned to look at him.

"Thank you for everything", Curtis said

Tania smiled "You're welcome. Now and always" he kissed her lightly on the cheeks before she alighted. Tania waited until he drove off and smiled contently, she was happy everything went well. She was about to turn and walk towards her apartment when she was held and dragged into an alley. Holding her by the jugular, he searched frantically for something in his hood pocket and proceeded to choke Tania. She was trying to breathe all to no avail. After some seconds, she was exhausted and was about to give in when she heard a loud bang. The assailant released her and she fell down with a thud, she struggled to breathe as the silhouette took to his heels, limping.

Tania opened her eyes to see people hovering all around her; she couldn't recognize them because her eyes were still hazy. After some seconds, she could recognize them. Standing close to her were people she valued; Lola, Sofia, Sarah, and her boss, Mr. Curtis Williams. But what's with the etheric smell, where is this place that she had found herself in?

"Heyyy" she slurred "what's happening?" her voice cracked

"Thank God!" Sarah exclaimed

Lola smiled "you passed out. We heard someone tried to attack you. A Good Samaritan intervened and called the ambulance. He explained that he hit the assailant with a golf stick"

Sofia hugged her right there on the bed "I couldn't believe my ears when I heard that my friend was admitted in a hospital. Thank God I found you alive" she said, hugging her tight

"Hey", Curtis said, smiling

"Hi", Tania said, her voice cracked. She was all smiles but she kept mute

After she was discharged, Curtis relayed the news to her about how his friend and fellow alderman, Walton Black was murdered in cold blood. She was dumbstruck

Curtis was in his new apartment, watching TV news. It was reported in the news that the mayor was arrested on a two count charge; money laundering and for the murder of Walton Black, the 5th Alderman of the city council. But his aide had escaped

The following week, Curtis' son was released from the state penitentiary after someone testified in court that he wasn't part of the crime gang. He was sent on rehab immediately after he was freed from incarceration. Curtis had gone to meet him and they reconciled.

Later that night, Curtis had gone to a café down the street for dinner and was strolling back to his apartment. As he was walking, his shoelace loosened. As he bent down to fasten it, he noticed a silhouette in the dark butdidn't think much of it. However, he noticed the figure kept moving nearer towards him. It was dark around that district and so he couldn't really fathom who the person was. He could hear siren blasting from a mile away. The silhouette figure seemed to be panting. Curtis decided to walk faster, but surprisingly the figure did. At a point, Curtis started running, the figure ran after him.

"Stop or I shoot!" the voice said

Curtis halted in his tracks and raised his hands up "Alright. But whoever you are, you don't have to pull the trigger, I am the 2nd alderman of the city council, I can …"

"Shut up!" the hooded figure thundered "I know who you are. You're Curtis Williams"

"Yes I am", Curtis stuttered, trying to turn around

"Stop trying to act smart, boy" the figure sneered

Curtis was terrified. Was this the end? Was this how he was gonna die? He thought. He knew he just had to say something to pacify his assailant

"I don't know who you are but I'm pretty sure we can talk about this", he stuttered

"There's nothing to talk about. He promised me your seat. I was to take over from you! You fucking ruined my chances! And now that my only chance of getting to the top has been dashed, I might as well shoot you for being a kill joy", he shouted

"FREEZE!" The voice disrupted the tension of the atmosphere. It was a policeman "Drop the weapon or I shoot!" he radioed his men for backup

"No I won't!" the hooded figure said

In a moment, a police van sped and screeched its tires to a halt. About five policemen jumped from the van with all alert as they pointed their guns at the assailant

"We know who you are, Mr. David Sanders. We've been searching for you for a week now. We know what you are up to. But you need not do that, just drop your weapons so we can settle this matter" one of the policemen spoke

The name sounded familiar to Curtis. And then it dawned on him that his assailant was the Mayor's aide.

"Drop your weapon now!" one of the policemen shouted

There was tension in the atmosphere for some seconds as the assailant thought between shooting Curtis and surrendering to the police.

KSHHHHH!!!

The bullet discharged with no forewarning

"That was Tania story and the Alderman".."It was a pathetic one!"
The minister got me a counselor and a lawyer for the rest of June and the whole of July. I was never allowed out of the renewal center. The counselor came weekly to the center to have sessions with me. My freedom was disallowed.

"Guess who got whipped today?" Wes ask me during dinner

"Who?" I asked

"Terry smith"

"Aww. Poor guy", I merely commented. Every Thursday, we all are to assemble at the hall around five to watch the pastor's weekly TV program. It was not optional, missing it meant you were going to be tied to a pole and get severely whipped, almost till you get pass out.

"D-man?"

"Huh?"

"You really should stop getting into trouble and the time!" he says amidst a mouthful

"Yeah, I know, I just can't help it sometimes. Guess what the counselor said was wrong with me to the minister?"

"He said you needed a haircut?" he joked.

"Well thanks, but I love afro". He said I was hyper because of the water"

"Wes bursts out in laughter," that's the craziest shit I've ever heard. But I'm sure that half-educated asshole would buy it"

"He sure did," I replied

"Well he should, maybe it would make him filter the water supplied to us since lead now makes people nuts", he laughs out again.

"But seriously, If that thing made one high, we should consider saving up the little cash we got and drink more water, marijuana and those narcotics are causing my pockets to dry up quickly all the time." I replied to the joke

"Speaking of narcotics, while you were still away in jail, some guys that were removed to have been planning another protest were thrown in jail". Wes said

"They just put them in jail like that?" No prove?"

"Of course, that wasn't gonna work, so their actual crime was having narcotics in their possession"

"What?" we got searched while coming inside and going out so how is it possible some people are able to smuggle contraband in?"

I'm as surprised as you are, so I believe they were set-up. Someone put those things in their stuff so as to get rid of them before they "Staged a mutiny" or committed "Treason," says Wes

"Frank fucking Albrights". I say

"Someone also must have led him to the place where they are sold", after a pause, he finally says, "I think its you"

"What?!" I was already getting mad

"Hey, dude, chill. I don't mean you betrayed us. I meant they could tracked you on GPS since you know all those ghetto places where shit like that got shared", he says suddenly frightened by my outburst

"Or, they could simply hired someone to buy the shit", I retort

"Whatever" he simply said. After a pause, he suddenly grabs my arm, a serious
Expression on his face, "Tonight we bursting otta here. No more postponing "

"Are you serious? Sure you ready for this?" I ask concerned

"Yes, dammit" one of pastor franks maid already told me this afternoon that his
body guards are gonna be off duty this night

"What if she's wrong?" I asked

"Then it's a do or die affair!"

"I'm with you brother". I grab hold of his arm as a sign promise narrator POV

At night ----10pm to be precise. Demarco is beginning to doze off. Wes is however
wild awake, contemplating when exactly to carry out his plan. He suddenly decides
"Demarco get ready". First, I need to take a peek!"

Demarco wakes up but misses the first past of Wes statement which he told him to
be ready. He however, hears Wes say he needed to use the bathroom. Shortly after
his bunk mate leaves Mr barnes comes in "Demarco!" he calls

"Jeez, you scared me man, what are you doing here by this time of the night? "

"where is your bunk mate?"

"He went to take a piss." He replied flatly

"well the minister would like to see you!"

"What for?"

"You ask him yourself"

"who calls another person by this time of the night?"

D-man asks rhetorically. Demarco follows behind Mr barnes as they leave the boy's home to the minister's house.

When Wes returns, he is surprised not to see Demarco "Already left?" I don't know D-man for being a coward. Maybe he's just waiting outside", he wonders.

He goes to call the rest—Leslie and Eric

"Ok guys, you know the plan. Eric, you follow outside. When I give the signal, you go in, press the fire alarm, and wait for everyone to run out. If the security at the gate is trying to come interfere, we erase him."

As soon as everyone is out "Leslie", you will go and set the place ablaze. Clear?

They all node to the plan. Leslie remains as Wes hands him a container of gasoline, while he holds on to the other, Wes and Eric both sneak-up on the mansion, the drunk pastor frank leaves his wife who was already fast asleep to attend to the waiting Demarco in his study.

"Demarco" he says slowly with a smile playing at his lips

"Come on, come give your father a hug!"

Demarco, already sensing the minister is boozed off, avoid him like a plague. "No, thanks"

"I will keep my hug to myself" why am u here? I asked

"The minster sighs and sits too close to D-man"

"I just feel we need a dialogue" he replies

"About?"

"You see, boys like you need men like us to be a team"..You need.."

"I'm otta here". Demarco starts to walk out when the minister grabs his arm and drags him back, pushing him to the floor.

The man quickly mounts him and reaches for his belt.

Demarco delivers him a punch from the side of his face. The minister lets out a scream, wincing in pain. Just at that same moment, a woman scream is heard downstairs. Eric and Wes had successfully burgled into the mansion without alerting any within about their presence.

The clueless lady emma could not answer for her husband's absence when asked where he was. Wes stabs her repeatedly in the torso while Eric stands guard. When he's done killing her, he runs out to wave a white piece of cloth to the already alert Leslie while Eric empties the gasoline everywhere in the house, just at the first floor. Eric hears the sound of broken glass above but ignores it. The now scared minister in his drunk state breaks a vase as he tries to retreat from approaching Demarco who has a bat in his hand.

He swings the bat at the minister who initially ducks but then has his head bashed in by a second swing. Possessed with anger, Demarco continues to hit the dead minister on with the bat till the thick smell of smoke hits him

Eric had emptied gasoline to as many rooms as possible after all the boys had ran out due to the fire alarm. He strikes a match and runs out and within seconds the renewal center was ablaze

"The fast approaching security men from the gate were knocked off unconscious by some of the orphans who were in support of the arson"

Eric and Wes approached the boys asking about Demarco

Trapped inside the burning mansion, Demarco is knocked off completely, haven choked on enough smoke.

Just then the fire reaches the second floor. The boys start to run away as the fire starts to spread.

"We have to go!" Eric tells Wes

"But D-man…"

"He was with the minister", Mr barnes shouts behind him, running towards the gate

"Fuck!" Wes spits out in frustration, starring back at the burning mansion in horror

THE END